For Kian, Louis, Wayne and Terry

First published in 2011 by Macmillan Children's Books
This edition published 2016 by Two Hoots
an imprint of Pan Macmillan
20 New Wharf Road, London N1 9RR
Associated companies throughout the world
www.panmacmillan.com
ISBN 978-1-5098-3659-8
Text and illustrations copyright © Emily Gravett 2011

1 3 5 7 9 8 6 4 2
A CIP catalogue record for this book is available from the British Library.
Printed in China

The illustrations in this book were created using oil based pencil,
watercolour and fire.

www.twohootsbooks.com

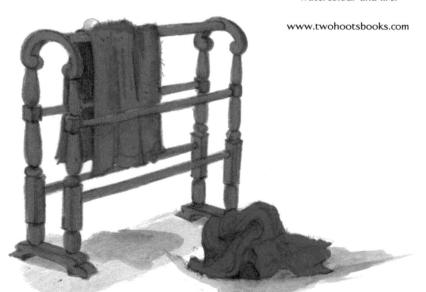

AGAIN

Emily Gravett

TWO HOOTS

For Kian, Louis, Wayne and Terry

First published in 2011 by Macmillan Children's Books
This edition published 2016 by Two Hoots
an imprint of Pan Macmillan
20 New Wharf Road, London N1 9RR
Associated companies throughout the world
www.panmacmillan.com
ISBN 978-1-5098-3659-8
Text and illustrations copyright © Emily Gravett 2011

1 3 5 7 9 8 6 4 2
A CIP catalogue record for this book is available from the British Library.
Printed in China

The illustrations in this book were created using oil based pencil,
watercolour and fire.

www.twohootsbooks.com

AGAIN!

Emily Gravett

TW🦉 HOOTS

It was nearly bedtime.

Cedric the dragon's a bright angry red.
He's never,
His whole life,
(Not once) been to bed.

At night-time when everyone else is asleep,
He noisily prowls through the tower, then leaps
Down to the bridge to be nasty and sly,
And torment the trolls (who by nature are shy).

When that makes him hungry he takes to the skies,
Grabbing princesses to turn into pies,
Or occasionally crumbles, or sometimes just toast
(If crumbles or pies would take too long to roast).

At the end of each day he shouts out this refrain:
"TOMORROW I'LL DO IT ALL OVER AGAIN!"

Again?

edric the dragon's a bright angry red.
He's never,
His whole life,
(Not once) been to bed.

At night-time when Cedric SHOULD be asleep,
He noisily stomps through the tower, then leaps
Down to the bridge to say a big sorry
For teasing the trolls (who do tend to worry).

When that makes him hungry he takes out a pie
Which he shares with the trolls. Then, heaving a sigh,
He goes home to his tower
And shouts out this refrain:
"TOMORROW I'LL DO IT ALL OVER AGAIN!"

AGAIN!

C edic the dragon's *a big sleepyhead.*
He's decided it's time
HE WAS REALLY IN BED.

He's made friends with the princess
And wished her goodnight,
The trolls are all happy,
The moon is out bright.

Now I'm closing the book and saying quite plain:

"TOMORROW I'll read it all over again."

2

AGAIN!

AGAIN!

Cedric the dragon is no longer red,

As Cedric . . .

the dragon's . . . asleep

. . . in . . . his . . . be . . . z z z   z

AGAIN!

AGAIN!

AGAIN!

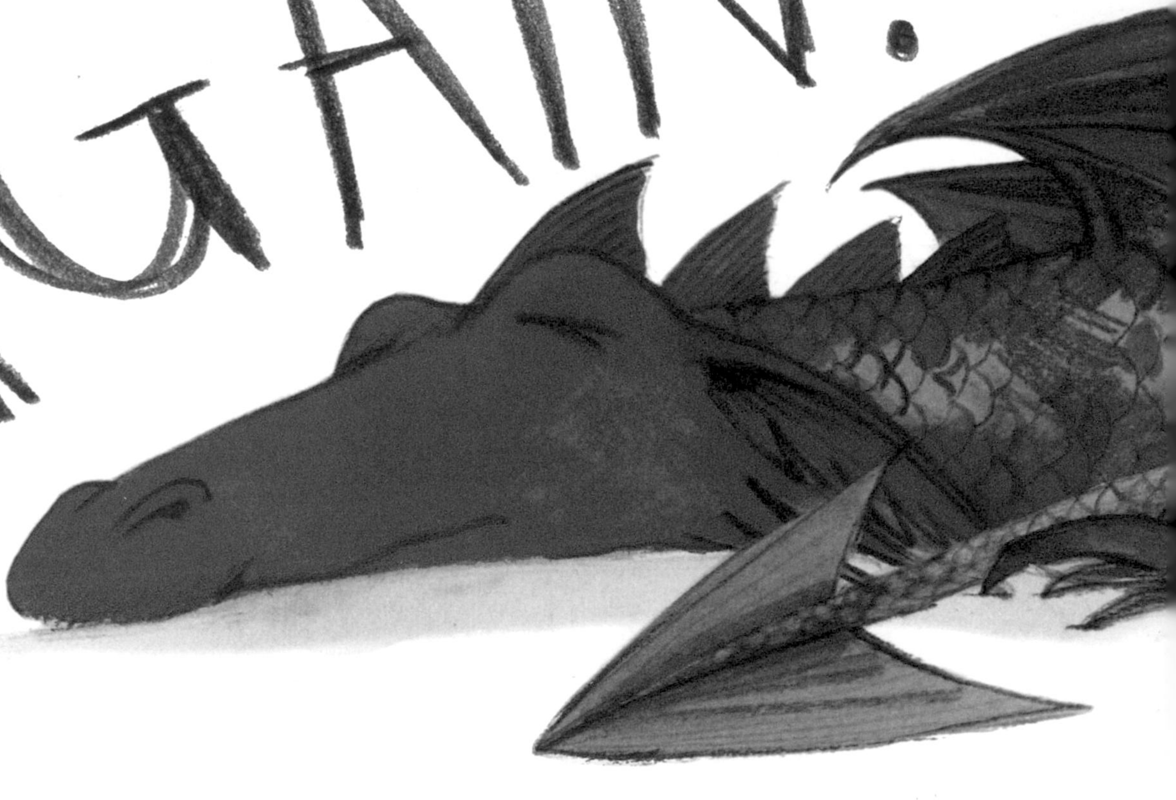

AGAIN! AGAIN
AGAIN
AGAIN
AGAIN AGAIN
AGAIN!